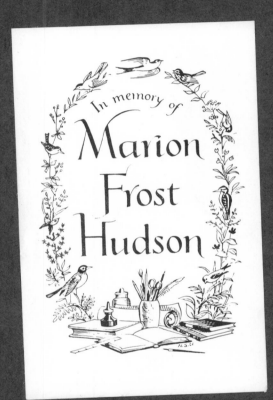

In memory of

Marion
Frost
Hudson

Owliver

by Robert Kraus

pictures by

Jose Aruego & Ariane Dewey

Windmill Books, Inc.
and E. P. Dutton & Co., Inc.
New York

Text copyright © 1974 by Robert Kraus
Illustrations copyright © 1974 by Jose Aruego
& Ariane Dewey   All rights reserved

Published simultaneously in Canada by Clarke,
Irwin & Co., Ltd., Toronto and Vancouver

Printed in the U.S.A.   First Edition
10 9 8 7 6 5 4 3 2 1

Library of Congress Cataloging in Publication Data

Kraus, Robert   Owliver

Summary: Although each one of his parents
expects him to be different things when he grows
up, a little owl makes up his own mind in the end.

I. Aruego, Jose, illus.   II. Dewey, Ariane, illus.
III. Title.
PZ7.K868Ou [E] 74-7232   ISBN 0-525-61526-1

For Augusta Baker,
who likes Owls

"I am an orphan."

"I have no father."

"I have no mother."

"I don't have anybody,"
said Owliver.

"Don't be silly," said Owliver's father.
"You do have a father."

"And a mother, too," said Owliver's mother.

"I know," said Owliver.
"I was just acting. I like to act."

Owliver acted all day.

Owliver acted all night.

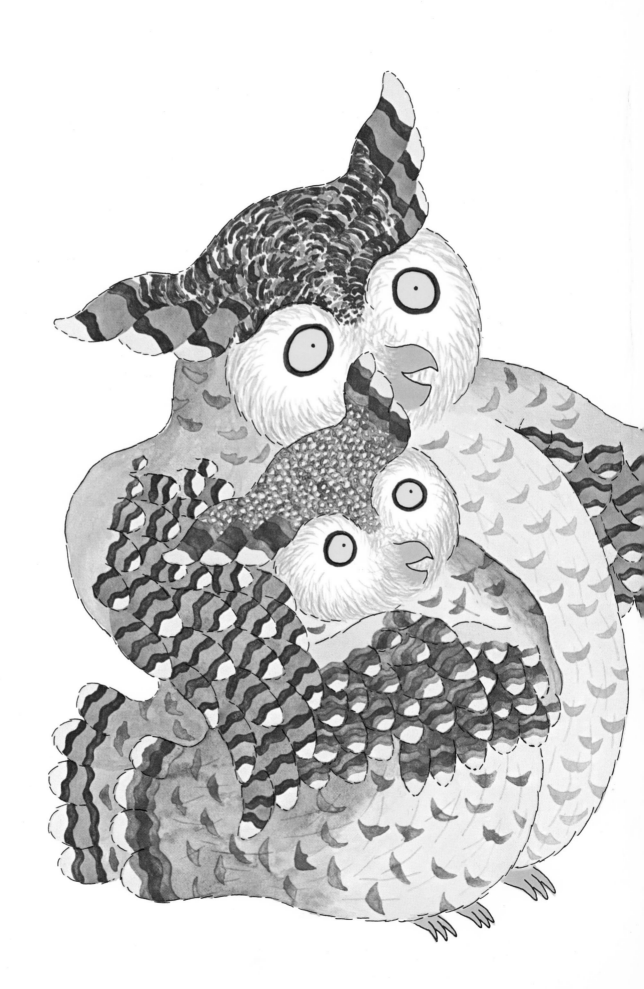

"Owliver is so talented,"
said Owliver's mother.
"Better he should be a lawyer or a doctor,"
said Owliver's father.

Owliver's father gave him doctor toys

...and lawyer toys.

Owliver's mother gave him acting lessons,

Joy

Anger

Fear

Sadness

Goodness

Hate

Love

...including tap dancing.
"Talent should be encouraged," she said.

Owliver acted out a play
about a doctor and a lawyer who never meet
(because Owliver played both parts).

And he pleased his mother
and he pleased his father.

"Owliver will become a doctor or a lawyer when he grows up," said Owliver's father.

"Owliver will become an actor or a playwright
when he grows up," said Owliver's mother.

But
   when
      Owliver
         grew
            up,
               guess what
                  he
                     became...

A FIREMAN!